To Fr. Justin,

Thank you for sharing your light and sharing your light and our school and parish community. You have helped all of us shine a little brighter and make this community a better place. Keep enjoying your journey — Shine On — *

Diane Carty Speicher ☺

10/11/04

 # 176/7500

D0536803

Brighton
ONE STAR'S JOURNEY TO SHINE

DIANE CARTY SPEICHER
illustrated by Lenord Robinson

SHINE ON! Publications
Brightening the heart of the universe one child at a time

Library of Congress Control Number 2004094683

ISBN 0-9749806-0-9

First Printing, 2005

Published in the United States by SHINE ON! Publications

Printed in Singapore

Brighton, One Star's Journey to Shine

Author: Diane Carty Speicher

Illustrator: Lenord Robinson

To Nicole and Chase,

…for being my shining stars and illuminating my life everyday.

To my beloved Dad,

…for inspiring me to dream the impossible dream and reach the unreachable star, and for teaching me, by example, how to shine.

To children everywhere,

…be the light that you want to see in this world, and then shine, shine, shine!

"Ideals are like stars; you choose them as your guides, and following them, you reach your destiny."

-Carl Schurz

Long, long ago,

in the galaxy called the Milky Way,

a very special star was born.

His name was Brighton.

This is the story of the most

amazing journey of his life.

CHAPTER *one*

It was the first time Brighton had ever been away from home, and he was excited. He was also nervous and scared. Home felt like it was light-years away. (In fact, it *was* light-years away!) He felt a little lonely, too. Even though he was surrounded by other stars, Brighton didn't know anyone at the North Star Academy.

"Throw it to me! Throw it to me!" he heard someone shout on the star field, where some young stars were playing a game of comet ball.

A young star with big glasses and a bow tie held the shining comet trying to decide where to throw it.

"No, throw it here! Throw it here!" another star shouted.

It sure looks like they're having fun, Brighton thought. He wished he could join them. But he was just a little star, so small and alone. He didn't know if he would ever find his place in the universe.

Brighton remembered the day he received his invitation to the North Star Academy. He was so excited his startips trembled as he opened the letter.

"Learn to fly faster and shine brighter than you ever have before!" the invitation had said. "We will light the way as you set off on exciting journeys and star quests to learn why your starlight is like that of no other star in the universe!"

But now that he was here, Brighton looked at the other young stars around him, each of them shining so bright. They all looked so confident and sure. Brighton wished he could shine with confidence, too.

Suddenly there was a loud roar, and all the young stars looked up to the sky. A rocket-shaped comet hurtled *wibbly-wobbly* toward the ground. With a *whoosh* and a *clank* and a flash of smoke and stardust, it came to a rickety stop right in front of them.

A small but shiny star, a white dwarf with a long mustache, climbed out of the cockpit and dusted himself off. It was Professor Nova, the headmaster of the North Star Academy, and the wisest star in the sky.

He looked around at all the students and in his loud, cheerful voice, greeted them with, "Shine On!"

Professor Nova led the students into the classroom. He waited until they were all seated and settled down, which seemed to take an eon. (In fact, it *did* take an eon!)

Finally the wise old star looked at them all, smiled and said,

"Star light, star bright,
The first star I see tonight!
I wish I may, I wish I might
Have my wish come true tonight!"

"This is why all of you are here," Professor Nova explained. "This is your life's purpose."

Brighton brightened with excitement. He was about to find out his place in the universe!

"Every night," the professor said, "millions and millions of children and animals on Earth look up into the sky and wish upon a star. Your job is to become bright enough to be seen by everyone everywhere, and to hear the wishes they make. And when you do…"

He paused, and Brighton leaned forward to hear what he was going to say next. What would happen when a star heard the wishes of a child?

"Energy and light and streams of magical stardust will flow through you," the professor said, his voice soft but powerful, "and you will be given the power to make those wishes come true."

All the stars in the room lit up.

"Wow!"

"Cool!"

"Awesome!"

"Your job as a young star," Professor Nova went on, "is to learn how to shine your very brightest light, and then share your light with others. Soon you'll be able to make wishes come true for anyone who asks!"

Brighton felt thrilled and scared, and he felt his insides flip upside down. Making wishes come true was such a great power. How on Earth would he ever learn how to do it? Would he be able to? He tried to imagine himself surrounded with energy and light and magical stardust, but he just couldn't do it.

"Starlight is a powerful thing," Professor Nova said, as if he were talking straight to Brighton. "It's the most powerful stuff in the universe. Whenever you're scared and things look grim, remember…*even a small amount of starlight can brighten the darkest night.*"

As he spoke, his words seemed to be made of light, and they traveled toward Brighton on a bright cloud.

"Even a small amount of starlight can brighten the darkest night."

Brighton closed his eyes as the *light message* surrounded him.

"Pssst…hey…," he heard someone whisper nearby.

Brighton opened his eyes and looked at the anxious young star sitting next to him. Brighton recognized him as the star he had seen playing comet ball before class. His bow tie and big round glasses made him look very smart.

"Do you think we're going to be tested on this?" the star whispered.

Brighton could only shrug.

Professor Nova wrote some words on the board, then quietly gazed upon them as though they were flowing into his heart. With a contented sigh he said, "The Light of All Lights makes all the stars in the universe shine. He is the Light you see way up in the sky, and the Light shining at the very center of your heart. He's the one who gave each and every one of you a purpose for being alive, a reason to shine. Talk to Him. Ask Him to guide you. He will be there to help you all your life long. He will help you shine your brightest light, if you let *His* light into your heart. No matter what happens, always remember to Shine, Shine, Shine!"

Time flew past, and Professor Nova taught them so much it made Brighton's head spin.

Finally, he said, "Now your homework is to think about a wish that you would like to grant with your light. Dream your biggest dream. Don't hold back. When you come back, be prepared to share your dreams with the class."

"Shine On!" he said to all the young stars as they flew out of the room.

The Light of All Lights

"My name is Bernie!" the star with the bow tie said to Brighton once they were outside. "Come on. I want you to meet my friends!" Bernie took Brighton to the star field and introduced him to Alphie, Leo, Proxy and Roxy.

"Pleased to meet you," said Alphie. She had shimmering red hair, which made it easy to spot her in the crowd. She was a very bright star who often amazed her friends with her brilliance.

"Grrr!" said Leo, growling and showing his teeth as he waved. Leo was going through his "lion" phase. He wore cool sunglasses and had spiked hair, and he wasn't afraid of anyone or anything.

"Hi!" said Proxy, with a friendly smile.

"Hmm!" said Roxy, looking Brighton over carefully.

Proxy and Roxy were twins, but their personalities were completely different. Proxy was open and friendly, while Roxy was much more cautious and sky smart. They were both warm and caring, but Proxy showed it while Roxy tried not to.

"Hey," said Leo, "want to play comet ball?"

"Sure," said Brighton.

"Will you be on my team?" asked Bernie anxiously.

"Of course," Brighton laughed. "I've known you longer than anyone!"

They played for the rest of that star-dappled afternoon. Brighton had never had more fun. For the first time in his life, he had friends.

They played for what seemed like ages. (In fact, it *was* ages!) Then Bernie accidentally threw the comet over Leo's head and it disappeared into a dark cloud of space gas.

"Sorry," said Bernie.

"Oh well," Alphie said lightly. "It was fun while it lasted."

"Why don't we go get it?" Brighton asked.

"No way!!! That's where the Black Hole Bullies live," said Proxy. "Even Leo won't go there."

Everyone knew about the Black Hole Bullies. They were the troublemakers of the universe. They were mean and angry, and could suck the brightness right out of any star. Dirty and smelly, they waited for the chance to make stars doubt their dreams.

Roxy shivered and said, "Once they get their starclaws in you, they pull and tug until you start to wonder if you really are a star at all!"

"Yeah," said Leo. "And I heard that if they throw you into their black hole dungeon, they can keep you prisoner for a super long time. Like five billion years!"

"Five billion years?" exclaimed Brighton. "That's halfway to forever, even for a star!"

"You want to hear the creepiest thing?" Alphie asked. "I heard that if you get sucked too far into a black hole, there's a point of no return called The Gravitron Zone. If you do enter The Zone you'll be spaghettified, which means you'll be stretched into long stringy bits until *SSSNAP!* you're torn apart into a million tiny pieces!"

All the stars were truly frightened by now. Brighton knew he had to say something. "Well, we just have to stay together and protect each other so that nothing like that ever happens to any of us!" he told them. "We are the Defenders of the Universe! We'll defend all good stars against the Black Hole Bullies!"

And with that, they all put their startips together and shouted, "Go Defenders! Shine On!"

The six stars laughed. Then they sat down and stretched out, looking up at the sky.

"So what's your biggest dream?" Alphie asked Leo. "Have you thought about the wish you want to grant?"

Leo nodded. "I want to grant the wish of a young lion cub to become a Lion King."

"I love that wish," said Proxy. "What about you, Bernie?"

"I think I'd like to grant the wish of someone who wants to grow up and invent medicine that will make sick people on Earth get well."

"How noble," said Roxy, dryly. "Maybe you'll win a prize."

"Well, what's your wish, then?" asked Bernie.

Proxy and Roxy looked at each other and giggled. Proxy spoke up for both of them. "We'd like to grant a pair of twins their wish to become stars—*movie* stars."

But as they all talked and laughed and shared their dreams, Brighton said nothing.

After awhile, Proxy noticed that Brighton was being very quiet. "How about you, Brighton?" she asked softly. "Do you have a dream?"

Brighton sighed. How could he talk about his dream, he thought, when he didn't think he could ever shine bright enough to make it come true? "Oh, I'm still thinking about it," he said.

While the others kept talking about their hopes and dreams, Brighton got up and flew away from the group. He had some thinking to do.

The truth was Brighton *did* have a dream, a *big* dream. He wanted to shine his brightest light so that he could grant a child his or her wish to grow up and teach people all over the Earth how to love one another.

But when he looked around the sky he could see billions and billions of stars. He felt like he was just one little star whose light was barely bright enough for even his friends to see.

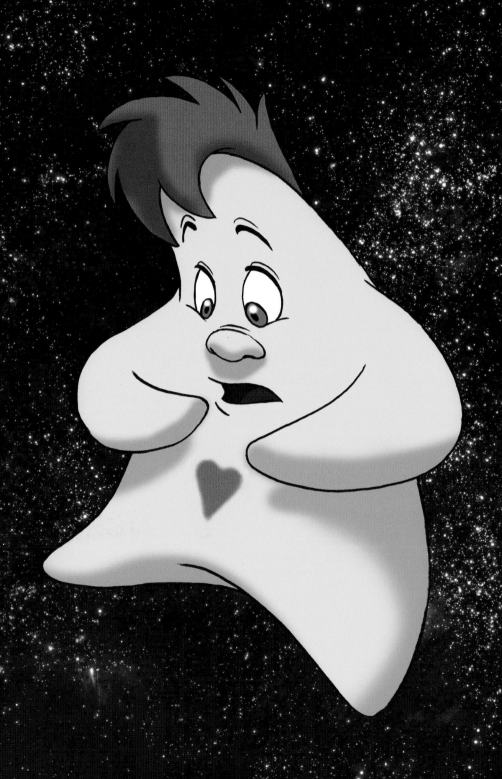

CHAPTER *three*

Brighton wandered, lost in his thoughts. And he wasn't watching where he was going. Suddenly he felt a small tug, then another. Then a big push sent him tumbling and spinning.

He tried to stop and stand up straight, but more tugs were coming now, stronger and faster. Was it a cosmic hurricane? A galactic tornado? He could see swirls of dark clouds closing in all around him.

Then he heard voices sneering and snickering.

"Hey, look what we've got here!" said one voice.

"It's a dumb little star!" said another.

"He lost his way, and now he's ours!" added a third.

The sky began to shudder with the sinister voices of the dreaded Black Hole Bullies—Scorfu, Hydrella and Darko!

Brighton's eyes widened as he saw the three huge, dark creatures with plumes of smoke and gas trailing behind them. His heart started racing and he felt sick to his stomach. Closer and closer they came. Brighton closed his eyes as the bullies yanked him from side to side and made loud, sucking noises. He felt like they could see right through him with their x-ray eyes.

Scorfu grabbed Brighton and pulled him up close until the two were eye to eye. Scorfu breathed dark, smelly gas all over the trembling star. Brighton felt his stomach turn upside down.

"What are you doing here?" Scorfu growled. "Who are you!?"

Brighton's heart was pounding and sweat was vaporizing on his face. As he started to speak his lips quivered. "I'm…I'm Brighton," he finally managed. "I'm one of the…um…one of the Defenders of the Universe."

Scorfu, Hydrella and Darko laughed so hard the sky shook.

"Defenders of the Universe?" Scorfu scoffed, shaking the little star. "You're the Defender of *Nothing*!"

Brighton could feel his light growing dimmer and dimmer by the minute.

Back at the North Star Academy, the other stars were still sitting and talking, when Bernie suddenly sat up straight. "Hey, where's Brighton?" he asked nervously.

The others looked around. Brighton was nowhere to be seen.

"He must have wandered off," said Proxy.

Then Alphie looked at the dark gas cloud where the Black Hole Bullies lived. There were flashes of light coming from inside. Something was happening.

"Look!" she shouted.

"You don't think he…," Leo began.

"No, he wouldn't have…," Roxy started.

"We've got to save him!" Alphie shouted, jumping to her feet. "We promised we'd help each other out, and now we've got to rescue Brighton! Remember what he said? We are the Defenders of the Universe!"

The five stars linked their startips and flew toward the black cloud at nearly the speed of light!

"ROAR!" roared Leo as the young stars flew into the dark cloud.

There was Brighton. And they could see he was in trouble. He was caught in a big tug of war between Scorfu and Hydrella.

"He's mine!" shrieked Hydrella.

"Let go!" screamed Scorfu.

The Black Hole Bullies just laughed as Hydrella and Scorfu kept pulling on Brighton's startips, stretching him further and further.

"*Both of you* let him go!" shouted Roxy, as the five young stars flew toward them.

"Who are you?" asked Darko, circling the group. "More Defenders of the Universe?"

"As a matter of fact, we are!" said Bernie, trying to put some conviction in his voice.

"Oh, we're *sooo* scared!" laughed Darko.

Suddenly there was a loud *SNAP* as Brighton's startip slipped out of Hydrella's fist. Brighton found himself whipping back toward Scorfu like a gigantic, solar-sized rubber band.

Scorfu growled when he saw Brighton heading straight toward him as fast as a shooting star. The bully let go of his startip at the last second, just in time to scramble out of the way.

"Hey!" Scorfu scowled as Brighton went whizzing past.

"Heeeeelp!" Brighton called to his friends as he sped far, far, far out into the universe, faster than their eyes could follow.

He disappeared into the vastness of space.

Brighton's friends couldn't believe it.

"Come on!" shouted Alphie. "We've got to go help him!"

But the Black Hole Bullies had other ideas.

"Grab them!" screamed Scorfu. Before the stars could move, the Bullies closed in.

Leo got so mad he couldn't think straight. Roaring, he made a fist and hurled a powerful punch at Scorfu's nose. Bernie grabbed Darko's tail, and Alphie jumped up to do a flying kick straight at Hydrella.

But the bullies just laughed. "You little dimwits!" Scorfu sneered. "You think you can win a fight with the Black Hole Bullies?"

With almost no effort, Scorfu, Darko and Hydrella turned the tables on the brave little stars. They grabbed Leo, Bernie and Alphie roughly by the shoulders and threw them into the black hole dungeon.

Proxy and Roxy could only watch in horror. "Nooo!" the twins screamed, as they saw their friends swirl around and around and around in the dark smelly gases of the dungeon and vanish into the deep, dark hole.

Then the Black hole Bullies turned to the twins, and closed in....

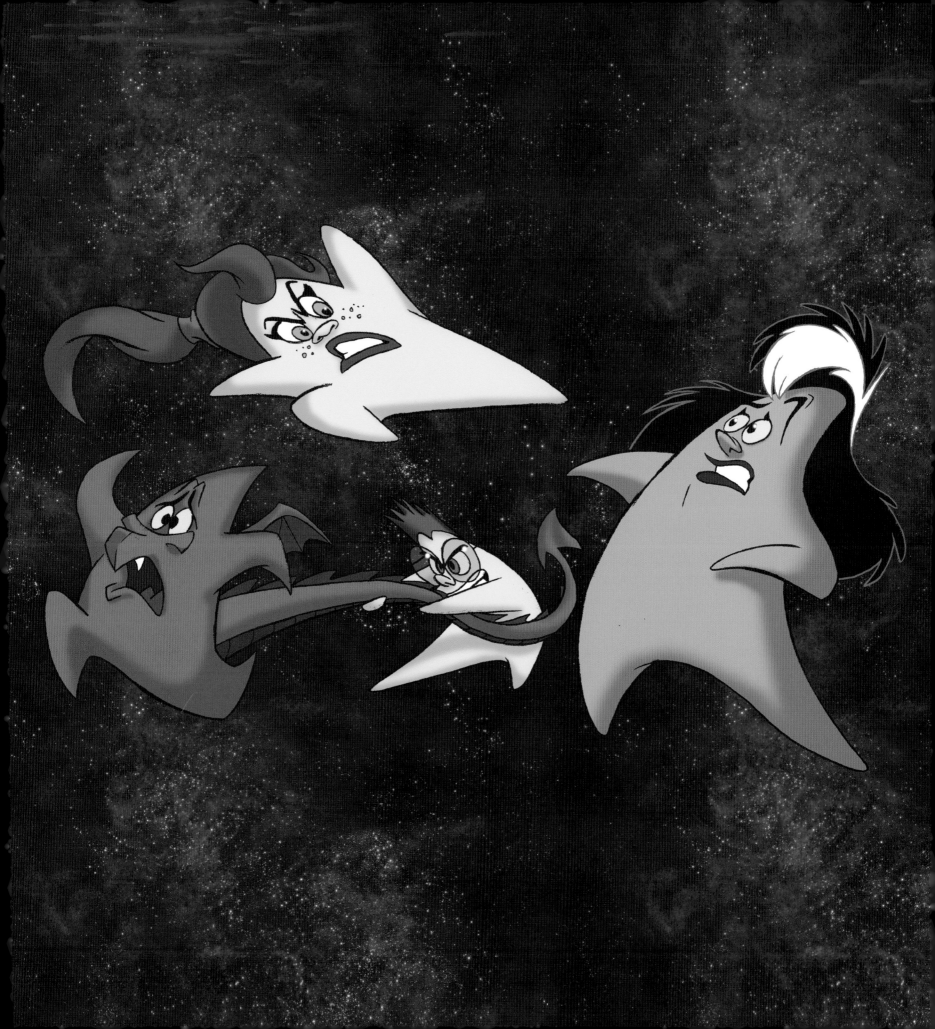

CHAPTER *four*

Meanwhile, Brighton sailed on and on through the sky. He felt like he was on a rocket ship destined for nowhere. His body felt achy, and he was dirty and smelly, too. *Yuck, yuck, yuck!* he thought.

As he sped past stars and asteroids and planets, Brighton put his startips together and said, "Oh, Light of All Lights, if you can hear me, I really, *really* need your help!"

All of a sudden—*KER-PLUNK!*—Brighton's flight came to an abrupt halt. He found himself nestled in the arms of a constellation he didn't recognize.

"Oh, you poor little star," a soothing voice said. "Look at you, all bruised and dirty. Don't you worry. I'll take good care of you."

It was the sweetest voice Brighton had ever heard. He looked up and saw a beautiful face surrounded by stars. "Who are you?" Brighton asked.

"My name is Virgo," the beautiful lady said, smiling down at him. "I'm the constellation other stars turn to when they've run into a bump or two along their journey. Here, let me clean you up."

"It looks like you've been through quite a scuffle," Virgo said. "Now where did I put my first aid kit?" After a moment, she found it. "Here," she said. "Let me put a bandage on your cut."

Virgo's touch was gentle, but Brighton's surface was bruised, and it stung as she cleaned him up.

"Ouch, that hurts," he said with a wince. "But only a little," he added, trying to sound brave.

"There you go," Virgo said, as she put a Starbright bandage on his wound. "Almost good as new!"

"Thank you for being so kind to me," Brighton said.

"But of course," Virgo answered. "That's what stars do."

Brighton stayed with Virgo while his wounds healed. They spoke about the North Star Academy, where many of the stars in Virgo's constellation went to school. And, with Virgo's encouragement, Brighton spoke about his dream of shining his brightest light for a special child on Earth.

"But I'm afraid that someone will always be standing in my way, like the Black Hole Bullies," he said. "After all, I'm just a low voltage star."

"But Brighton," Virgo replied, "*the only one who can stop you from fulfilling your dream is you.*"

It seemed to Brighton that the words themselves were written light.

> *The only one who can stop you from fulfilling your dream is you.*

After he had absorbed this *light message*, Virgo continued. "The Black Hole Bullies can't stop you, nor can anything else in the universe. Others may try, but only you can control your destiny. If you believe in yourself, and in the gift of light you carry in your heart, you will be able to do anything your heart can dream of."

When Brighton was completely healed, Virgo unrolled a map—a very large map. "This is where we are," she said, pointing to one corner of the map. "And this is where you want to go," she went on, tracing the route with her finger. "Think you'll be able to find your way?"

"Sure!" said Brighton, excited to be heading back.

"Then good-bye, Brighton," Virgo said, smiling. "If you run into trouble, other stars will be there to guide you on your way. And always remember to share your light with others, but never let anyone extinguish yours!"

"I'll remember!" said Brighton, waving good-bye.

CHAPTER five

*P*hew, *it seems like I should be there by now*, Brighton said to himself, half out of breath. He slowed down a little, and looked around at all the millions of stars he passed as he floated through the sky. They all seemed so bright. He had trouble imagining he could ever shine like they did. What was even worse, he noticed that every time he doubted himself, his light grew a little dimmer—which only made him worry more. Poor Brighton began to wonder if he had enough light left to get himself back to the academy.

Just then, he saw a constellation of stars up ahead that looked a little familiar. He realized it was the famous constellation he admired every night before he went to bed. *Maybe I could stop by and borrow a little light*, Brighton thought. He decided to pay a visit.

"Um, er, excuse me," Brighton stammered. "My name is Brighton. Aren't you the Big Dipper?"

"Well, hello, Brighton! Come on in and have a seat. My real name is Great Bear. But you're right, most people know me by my family name, which is Big Dipper. This is my younger brother, Little Bear, also known as Little Dipper."

"You can call me Little Dipster, if you'd like. That's what all my friends call me," added the youngster.

"It's just amazing to meet you both face to face. You're just so…so…*BIG* and *so BRIGHT*. I bet everyone on Earth can see you!" Brighton smiled politely, then asked, "Is there any way I can borrow some of your light?"

"Well, no, that's not possible," the Big Dipper responded, "because no one can ever shine anyone's light but their very own."

Brighton was disappointed, but he tried not to show it. Knowing he couldn't borrow any light from the Big Dipper made him think he'd never shine as brightly as he wanted to. He grew discouraged, making his light grow even dimmer.

"What's the matter, my young friend? You seem to be fading away before our very eyes. Would you care to tell us your trouble?"

Brighton told his new friends everything—about his lessons at the Academy, his run-in with the Black Hole Bullies, his visit with beautiful Virgo, and his journey back to the Academy. Then he said, "Every time I see how bright and beautiful the other stars in the universe are, I feel smaller and dimmer myself. What can I do?"

"Brighton, there's something you should understand," the Big Dipper replied. You see, *we're all different with our own very special talents.*"

As the Big Dipper said the words, Brighton saw them all lit up in a cloud that settled around his shoulders. He immediately felt better, and his light began to grow brighter. He knew the Big Dipper had given him another *light message*.

We're all different with our own very special talents.

"My younger brother can tell you a story that will help you understand," said the Big Dipper.

The Little Dipper began. "When I was younger, I was really jealous of my older brother. After all, he's the Big Dipper and I'm so much smaller than he is. He had more stars in his constellation than I did, and I thought that made him bigger and brighter and stronger and better. I didn't like that, and so late at night I would sneak over to his constellation, grab a few stars and bring them back to mine. I did this over and over again for a few weeks, until I became bigger and brighter. I thought that would make me feel really happy, but you know what? Even though I was brighter on the outside, I felt miserable on the inside."

"And then what did you do?" Brighton asked, eager to hear the rest.

"I gave my brother back every one of the stars I had taken," Little Dipper answered. "And then I cried and cried and cried."

"That's when I stepped in." said the Big Dipper. "I put my arm around him and told him that life is not a competition. We weren't born to try to outdo each other. We were born simply to be the best we can be, and to share our gifts of light with one another."

"And you know what I discovered then?" asked Little Dipper with excitement in his eyes.

"No, what?" Brighton asked.

"I discovered that at the tip of my constellation was the North Star! *The North Star*! In *my* constellation—not my brother's, not Virgo's, not Orion's…but *mine*! I was so busy trying to steal my brother's light that I hadn't even noticed my own brightest light. Unbelievable, isn't it? That's why I always tell other stars that each and every one of us has something unique and special that we were born with. We just need to make the most of the gifts that we've been given."

Brighton enjoyed his time with the Little Dipper and the Big Dipper, but he was feeling much better, and he knew it was time to move on. He said his good-byes, then off he flew, out into the night sky, eager to go home and share all he'd learned with his friends.

Brighton raced across the sky, and had almost reached the North Star Academy. But he had to stop one last time to catch his breath. Suddenly, he saw the most dazzling light he had ever seen. He flew closer to get a better look.

It was Sirius, the brightest star in the sky. She was so beautiful she looked like an angel.

"Well, you're a bright little star," Sirius said to him. "What brings you here to visit me?"

Brighton could hardly speak. "Your light is so beautiful," he finally managed to say. "What can I do to become bright like you, so I can grant a wish for a child on Earth?"

Sirius was moved by Brighton's plea and she could tell by the look on Brighton's face that he was almost ready to shine.

"There's only one more thing you need to learn," she said. "*Have the courage to let the Light of All Lights shine through you, and then turn around and share that light with all the world.*"

Once again, these words seemed to be written in light.

Have the courage to let the Light of All Lights shine through you, and then turn around and share that light with all the world.

"Once you do that," Sirius continued, "you will be guided from above and your dream will unfold."

Brighton felt so much warmth and love in her presence, he didn't want to leave. But he knew he had to go. "Thank you, Sirius," he said, giving her a big hug, and then he headed out into the universe, back to his friends and the Academy.

CHAPTER *six*

Brighton flew all the way back to the North Star Academy, his heart racing. He was eager to share all he'd learned with his friends. But when he got there, the school was deserted. He went from classroom to empty classroom.

"Hello!" he called. "Is anyone here?"

Then he heard something. It sounded like muffled voices trying to call out. Brighton went around the corner—and there he saw Proxy and Roxy, their startips tied behind their backs, and small asteroids stuffed in their mouths.

"What in the space-time continuum happened?" Brighton asked as he quickly untied the twins.

"The Black Hole Bullies!" said Proxy.

"They captured all of our friends!" said Roxy.

"And then they went around the school, and sucked everyone into their black hole dungeon!"

"They even got Professor Nova!"

Brighton was getting more and more frightened.

Then Proxy looked him straight in the eye. "They only left us here," Proxy said, "because they knew you'd come back to find us. They're after you, Brighton. They know you're a bright star, and they don't want you to shine."

"Me?" said Brighton, surprised. "A bright star?"

"One of the brightest," said Roxy.

Brighton didn't know what to say. And he was scared. He didn't want to face the bullies again, but he knew he couldn't leave his friends in the dungeon.

Maybe, he thought, *just maybe, with everything I've learned*…and in his mind, he heard the *light message* that Professor Nova had taught him:

Even a small amount of starlight can brighten the darkest night.

…even the darkness of the Black Hole Bullies!

He remembered the *light message* he'd learned from Virgo:

The only one who can stop you from fulfilling your dream is you.

The bullies couldn't force him into their dungeon, no matter how many mean things they said or how bad they smelled, as long as he believed in the brightness of his own light.

And he remembered what the Big Dipper had told him:

We all have our own very special talents.

Suddenly it all made perfect sense. All Brighton and his friends had to do was use their own special talents. If they did, the Black Hole Bullies didn't stand a chance!

"I'm not running away from them," Brighton told Proxy and Roxy. "They don't control me, and they don't control anyone else. Let's go rescue our friends!"

Brighton felt stronger and braver and brighter. Hope radiated from every startip. "Remember, we are the Defenders of the Universe!" he shouted. "Shine On!"

Brighton had a plan. He and the twins went zooming across the sky to see the beautiful planet Saturn.

"Wow!" Proxy gasped. "Look at her bright rings! Purple, green, blue and gold!"

"She's incredible," Roxy said.

"Welcome," said Saturn. "I love visitors. What brings you here?"

Brighton quickly told Saturn everything the Black Hole Bullies had done. Then he said, "We're here to ask you a *big* favor. Can we borrow some of your rings to help us rescue our friends?"

No one had ever asked Saturn if they could borrow her rings before. But she admired Brighton's *chutzpah*.

"Take them," Saturn said. "As long as you promise to use them to save your friends and make the universe a brighter, more joyful place, you're welcome to all you need."

Brighton and the twins gathered up armloads of rings and flew back to the Black Hole Bullies' deep, dark, swirling hole in the sky.

"Hey Scorfu, Darko, Hydrella!" Roxy called. "Look who we found!"

"Brighton is back," sang out Proxy.

Scorfu, Darko and Hydrella crept out to see what all the noise was about.

Roxy swooshed past the Black Hole Bullies. "We are the Defenders of the Universe!" she shouted, "and we will shine our light on all the dark places in the world!" As she swooshed, she let out a trail of golden lightbeams.

"Wow!" said Proxy. "I didn't know you could do that!" Then Proxy zoomed as fast as she could straight toward Scorfu, and stopped right in front of him. She spread out her startips and spun on one starpoint as she began to flicker her heart light on and off, on and off. "I can make dreams come true!" she shouted with joy.

Scorfu, Darko and Hydrella were stunned. They didn't expect this! They thought the Defenders of the Universe would fight with kicks and punches and jumps, like they had before. The Black Hole Bullies *always* won those kinds of fights. But fighting with love and laughter and starlight??? What good was a little stinky old breath and a dungeon against weapons like that?

The twins held hands and danced closer and closer to the bullies. Roxy and Proxy were spinning and twirling so fast, all the bullies could see were stars in their eyes. They got dizzy and teetered back and forth. The pair giggled and whirled with delight as they realized they were actually winning the battle.

But the Black Hole Bullies fought back. They pulled and tugged and pulled again, as hard as they could at the bright and shiny twin stars, but Proxy and Roxy just slipped away every time.

"Watch out!" yelled Proxy.

"Don't let them suck in your light," yelled Roxy. "Remember what Professor Nova said! *Shine, Shine, Shine!*"

The girls laughed and kept dancing. "Hey Scorfu, Hydrella, Darko!" they shouted gleefully. "Come and see what we can do!"

They began to fly back and forth and back and forth, creating big arches in the sky, one right on top of the other, until there were seven perfect arches. Then they stood back and, with a whoosh

of their startips, filled in each arch with a color. Red! Orange! Yellow! Green! Blue! Indigo! Violet! It was the most beautiful rainbow the universe had ever seen!

The Black Hole Bullies saw the beautiful colors and felt sick to their stomachs. They hated bright lights, and they detested bright colors even more.

"YUCK! YUCK!" groaned Scorfu.

"Eeeuw, triple YUCK!" cried Darko.

"How dare they show up and shine those lights around here?!" snapped Hydrella, stomping her feet.

But while they tried to sound brave, all three bullies felt weaker and sicker with every colorful flash of starlight.

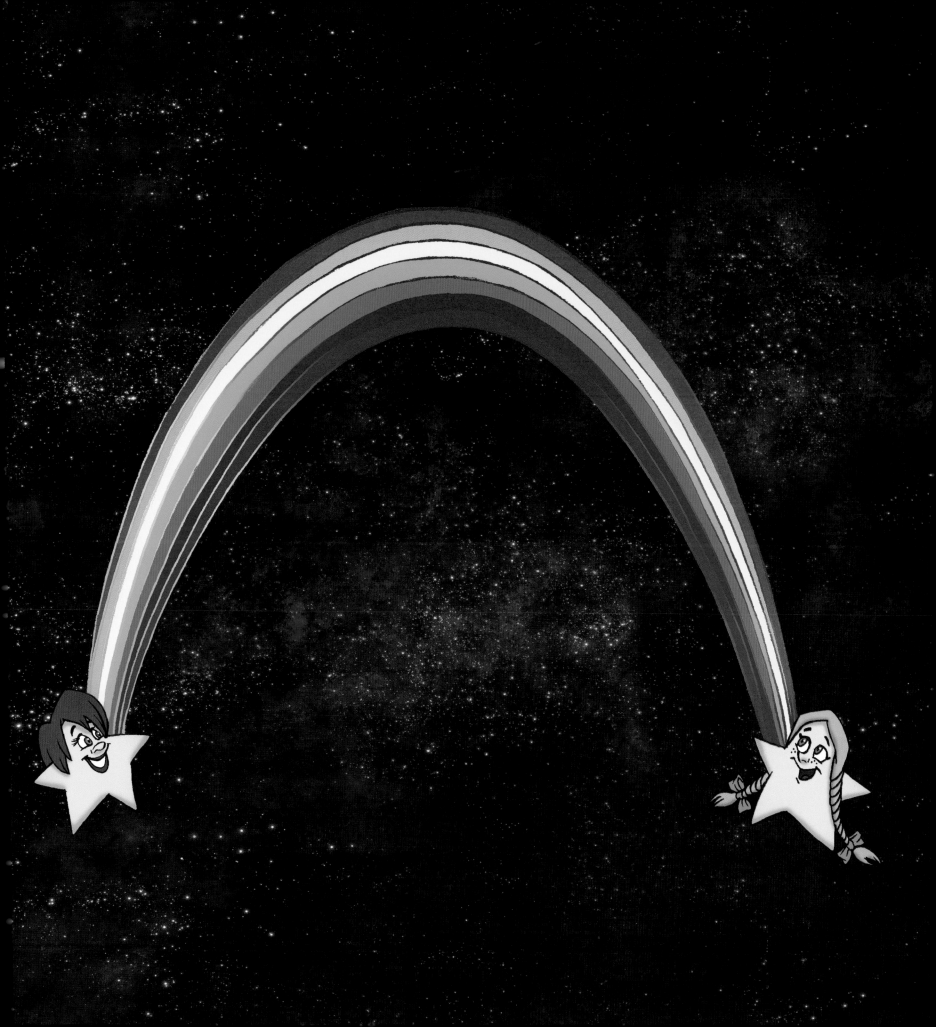

"Come on," Hydrella said to the others. "We can't let these girls beat us!"

The three Black Hole Bullies tried one more time to capture the twins. But Proxy and Roxy continued to dance and twirl, flashing light and sprinkling stardust at the bullies.

Scorfu, Darko and Hydrella tried harder. They circled the twins, taunting and teasing. They came closer and closer until they were face to face.

"Come on, you weak little girls," Darko taunted. "It's time to experience the darkness. Your light is about to be extinguished!"

"Not if I have anything to say about it," shouted Brighton, as he snuck up from behind. He swung Saturn's rings around the bullies and tied them up together in a knot.

As he did, the twins shot straight up in the air, laughing and scattering starbeams.

"You'll never get away with this!" yelled Scorfu. "You're still just a dim good-for-nothing star who will fail, fail, fail!"

Proxy, Roxy and Brighton grinned at each other. They put their startips together and shouted, "*Shine On!*"

And off they flew. They looked back to see the Black Hole Bullies looking mighty defenseless, all wrapped up in Saturn's rings, their scruffy hair flapping in the solar wind.

CHAPTER *seven*

The three young stars headed straight for the Black Hole Dungeon to rescue their friends, but they had a tough job ahead of them. Even with the bullies out of the way, Brighton knew the pull of the dungeon was so strong, there was a danger they could all be sucked into it.

So he took one of Saturn's rings and handed it to the strongest constellation in the sky.

"Hercules," Brighton said, "I need you to hold onto this ring really tight. Don't let go no matter what!"

"They don't call me Hercules for nothing!" Hercules replied in his deep, booming voice. "No one in the entire universe can match my strength! Happy to help out!"

While Hercules held onto one end of the ring, Brighton stretched it into a long, colorful rope and lowered himself deep into the black hole dungeon. Proxy and Roxy followed close behind.

It was dark and cold inside, but Brighton could see hundreds, maybe thousands of pairs of eyes peering out from the dungeon. He let his light illuminate the dark, cold space.

Alphie, Bernie, Leo and Professor Nova were the first prisoners to spot their friend, and they flew over to give him a bug hug.

"It's so great to see light again!" Leo exclaimed.

"And wonderful to be warm, too!" Alphie said with a shiver.

Brighton climbed up on an asteroid and called out to the other prisoners. "Listen up, everyone!" he began, as they all gathered around. "I know the Black Hole Bullies have been telling you that your light is worthless, that it's too dim for anyone to see, and that no one in the universe cares about you.

"Well, I'm here to tell you that your light *is* valuable and you *are* important—each and every one of you! Children and animals all around the universe need you to shine your light. They want you to give them hope that their wishes will come true. Some of them may need you to just listen to what's in their hearts.

"Whatever it is, your light is important. *Don't ever forget that! You are worthy, and you deserve it!*"

Wow! Brighton was amazed to see a *light message* float out of his mouth.

You are worthy and you deserve it.

This must mean something, he thought, unaware that he was getting closer to fulfilling his dream.

"Those of you who are ready to twinkle, sparkle, dazzle and shine—let's go!"

Cheers of celebration rang out all around, as one by one the stars held on to the colorful rope and pulled themselves out of the dungeon. Some cried tears of joy as they flew out into the warm and beautiful night sky. Others danced and sprinkled stardust as they flew off to take their places in various corners of the universe.

When the last star had left the dungeon, Brighton held on tight to Saturn's ring and checked to make sure all of the stars had made it out safely. Then he made his way past the Black Hole Bullies and into the sparkling sky.

Once everyone was out, Brighton and his fellow Defenders of the Universe pushed the bullies into their dark dungeon. Then Hercules covered the entrance with a huge asteroid.

"That should take care of them for now!" Hercules declared. "I'll come back in an eon or two to see if they've decided to change their ways. In the meantime, they'll no longer be a menace to the universe."

But deep within the dark hole, the Black Hole Bullies had a different idea.

"We're not going to give up until Brighton is ours!" Scorfu spat angrily to his cohorts. "Maybe he beat us this time, but in the end, we will win!"

CHAPTER *eight*

Back at the North Star Academy, Professor Nova held a special ceremony to honor Brighton for being a hero. He placed a medal around the young star's neck. He also gave medals to Proxy and Roxy, and the other Defenders of the Universe, for their bravery.

Brighton was beaming.

"Have you noticed how much brighter you have become, Brighton, since this ordeal began?" Professor Nova asked.

Brighton hadn't noticed. But when he looked down at himself, he could see that he was a whole lot brighter. Brighton couldn't believe it. He was so bright, he was dazzling!

"You have become brighter because you believed in yourself," Professor Nova explained. "And you shared your gifts and talents with others."

Professor Nova smiled. "Go now, Brighton. Go. It's time for you to fulfill your dream."

Brighton was so excited he threw his arms wide open, and out through his startips streamed the most incredible fireworks display his friends had ever seen!

Brighton went higher and higher, up into the sky.

"Yes," he said out loud. "I'm ready."

Or am I? he thought, as his old doubts crept back into his heart.

And then he remembered the final *light message* he'd learned, the one Sirius had given him:

> *Have the courage to let the Light of All Lights shine through you,*
> *And then turn around and share that light with all the world.*

Brighton found himself a nice, cozy place in the sky. He stood there, peaceful and still, admiring the beauty surrounding him.

And then he began to pray. "I'm ready, Light of All Lights," he said. "I'm ready to shine my light and share it with others. Just lead me to where you want me to go and I will follow."

In the stillness of that night, Brighton heard a voice within that said,

It's your time, Brighton, time to shine brighter than you ever have before. Do not be afraid, for my light will always be with you, shining deep inside your heart.

Brighton began to dance and twirl through the sky. He whirled past constellations, planets and stars. He had no idea where he was going, but he knew he was being guided by a light far greater than anything he had ever known before.

Soon he felt himself slowing down, until he finally stopped in a quiet and peaceful spot in the sky. He felt energy and light and streams of magical stardust surge through his body. He was glowing, and light was radiating from every one of his startips. He felt happy, peaceful and humbled, all at the same time.

Brighton looked down and realized his light was shining brightly on a beautiful blue planet. He moved closer and saw that, lo and behold, his dream of shining his brightest light for some special child on Earth, someone who wished to grow up and teach people all over the Earth how to love one another, was unfolding before his eyes.

Brighton took a deep breath and whispered, "Thank you, Light of All Lights."

Then he began to let all of the light from deep inside his heart shine on…

...to one very special child
lying in a humble little barn at the edge of town.

And on that night, Brighton realized that the journey in search of his brightest light led
him to a destination far greater than anything he could have ever imagined for himself.

THE END...
...and the beginning

We'd love to hear from you!

Do you have a story that you would like to share with us? If so, we might use it in a future book from SHINE ON! Publications to help other children shine their brightest light.

For example:
How do you want to use your starlight?

What is your biggest dream?

Maybe you have a story about your own black hole bullies. Do they appear as doubts that you have in yourself?

Or have you encountered real life bullies who try to make you feel less wonderful than you are?

How have you succeeded in 'overcoming' your black hole bullies?

Please send us your stories:

12325 Kosich Place
Saratoga, CA 95070

or log on to *www.shineonpublications.com* and e-mail your story to us at *stories@shineonpublications.com*

The writing and publishing of this book has been nearly a four-year journey for me. Along the way, I have had the love, support and guidance from many wonderful people. I'd like to take a moment to acknowledge and thank them.

T h a n k

Bob, Nicole and Chase

Thank you for believing in me and in the story of Brighton. Your dedication and patience has been invaluable, and your pride in this body of work is very much appreciated. Having you in my life makes me want to shine brighter than I ever thought imaginable. I look forward to sharing the next part of the journey with you.

Colby

To my wonderful, loyal, furry companion. Your unconditional love is priceless.

Sheldon Borenstein

I was lucky to have found such a gifted artist to help me create all of the characters and a few key illustrations. The light is truly in your hands.

Lenord Robinson

You are so talented. You helped bring to life images that were inside of my head and put them so creatively in animated scenes. Your hands and heart shine.

Jan Allegretti

Thank you for guiding me to become a better writer. You've helped me create a final manuscript that I could let go of with confidence and faith. Your soul shines.

Eric Elfman

It has been wonderful working with you. Your editing expertise has helped to make this book better than ever. Thank you for sharing your gift of writing with me.

Cintara Corporation
Lisa Tollner-Sliva, Marni Zampa, Rachelle Orosa, Chris Canote— You have done an incredible job laying out the book. Your attention to detail has been invaluable. I look forward to working on many more projects with you.

Jack Canfield
Thank you for believing in this story and in my passion for wanting to share the spiritual messages with the world. Your endorsement of this book is invaluable to me, and I will be forever grateful.

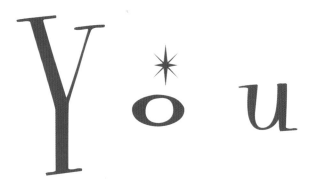

Gloria Speicher
Your involvement with this book has been priceless. I am fortunate to have had your insight and input. Thank you so much.

Carol Simone
You are my spiritual mentor, and one of my wisest teachers. You have encouraged me to live up to my potential and I thank you.

Betty Boyce
Four years and hundreds of manuscripts later, I have finally got it right! Thank you for your encouragement from day one to write on!

John Thompson, Ruth Thompson and Judy Morrow
Thank you for your editing input as well. Every little bit helps, and your comments were valuable to me.

Susan Keck
Thank you for the lyrics and music that Brighton inspired you to write, and for your kind heart and powerful prayers.

The Maui Writers Conference, The Christian Writers Conference, The Big Sur Children's Writer's Workshop, C.L.A.S.S. and the CBA
Thank you for organizing outstanding conferences where I learned so much about the craft of writing, publicity and promotion, and gained an enormous amount of knowledge of the publishing world. I look forward to a lifetime of learning.

Sandy Carty
Thank you for believing in me and in this book, and standing by my side when I needed support. I cherish your love and pray that you dazzle us with your light for many, many more years to come.

To all of the Carty, Galloway, Testa, Consorti, Speicher, Gaspar and Silva families
Family is so important to me. Thank you for the patience and support that you've given me over the years. I love you all, and look forward to sharing the next part of my life's journey with you.

To all of my wonderful friends
Thank you for the gift of friendship, love, support and encouragement that I get from each and every one of you. I appreciate and love you all.

To the students at St. Mary's School and the children of the parish, both past and present
Guiding you to believe in yourself and in the light you carry inside has lead my light to shine even brighter. Keep shining!

To Grandma Sanderson
Your beautiful light is still shining here with us after nearly 103 years! Thanks for instilling in my mom a lifetime of faith that she passed on to me.

To my beloved late Grandma Mary
We were so fortunate to have shared your wise and precious light for nearly 100 years. To me, you are Sirius, the brightest star in the sky. I know you have been with me through this journey, and I love you.

To my beloved late Dad
Words cannot describe how much I loved, honored and cherished you, and continue to do so now. You were the greatest father, teacher, mentor, role model, hero and friend to me. I wish you could have seen this completed Brighton book, but I know in my heart and soul that you are well aware of it now, and that your light will guide this book, and me, to all we're meant to be. I keep looking up in the sky and seeing your star, Dave Carty Star 73, shining down on me. Thanks for all of your past, present and future support. I'll love you forever into eternity, Dad. Shine On!

To God, my eternal Light of All Lights
Thank you for being my co-author and partner in this book, and in my life. I am so grateful, everyday, for all of the wonderful gifts you have given me. Help me to stay the course and to fulfill my life's purpose. I pray for your continued guidance that I may help light the way for others to shine brighter than they ever have before and make this world a brilliant place in which to live.